Tweedle & Dee

Written & illustrated by
K.J. Knight

 FriesenPress

Suite 300 - 990 Fort St
Victoria, BC, v8v 3K2
Canada

www.friesenpress.com

ISBN
978-1-5255-8350-6 (Hardcover)
978-1-5255-8349-0 (Paperback)
978-1-5255-8351-3 (eBook)

Juvenile Fiction, Animals

Distributed to the trade by The Ingram Book Company

Dedicated to my grandson, Theodore, and

all the children everywhere

who are learning to

adjust to a different world around us.

Trust those you love to keep you safe.

Stay close to home little buddies

and wash your paws.

2020

Once upon a time in a forest lush and green,

lived two little bears and

their little friend Peep.

Brother bear Tweedle and sister bear Dee,

played in the grass and loved running free.

These two little bears were just having fun,

when Tweedle yelled, "Hey, sister, come quickly! Run!

Tweedle, it seemed had found something great.

something sweet and delicious! he just could

not wait.

Dee came a running as quick as could be,

To see what Tweedle had found in the tree.

Peep flew ahead and looked to the sky,

the treasure he saw, he knew was too high.

Up on the branch in the big old tree,

A honey pot hung as sweet as could be.

Their eyes on the goodness,

their feet off the ground.

They climbed and they climbed to the treasure

they found

Little bears climb but little bears fall,

now these little bears picked a tree too tall.

Little Peep circled cause Little Peep knew,

he flew to their Mama; she'd know what to do!

They got to the honey and as sure as could be,

along came the Queen with her little honeybees.

"Yikes!" said Tweedle and "Yikes!" said Dee,

we do not know how to get out of this tree!

Now the bees were a buzzing, and they headed for Dee.

Now the two little bears were as scared as could be.

Stuck in the tree too far from the ground,

and more angry bees kept coming around.

"Help!" cried Tweedle and "Help!" cried Dee,

"Mother please get us down and out of this tree!"

Then out of the blue came a sound drawing near,

a voice so familiar, a face oh so dear.

A flutter of wings and a pounding of feet,

their mother was following their little friend Peep.

Well Mama came running and zipped up the tree,

then down came Tweedle and down came Dee.

Now sitting with mama and thinking things through,

These little bears learned a lesson or two.

True friends will help you with trouble and fear,

but Mama is best to always stay near.

 KIMBERLEY KNIGHT is a Canadian children's author who has enjoyed writing short stories and poetry for many years. Her love for forests and all its creatures has inspired her to create her first published children's story "TWEEDLE AND DEE'" which she wrote and illustrated. She has cared for children for over 20 years in a daycare setting and loved to teach about nature and the world around them. With a passion for drawing, writing and photography, she looks forward to a future with more time for her creative projects. Kimberley lives in Winnipeg with her family, an enchanting garden, and an infinite collection of sewing projects. She believes that in every day you should find a moment for joy.

CPSIA information can be obtained
at www.ICGtesting.com
Printed in the USA
BVHW091043111120
593059BV00014B/1153

9 781525 583490